When I am with Dad

written by

Kimball Crossley

illustrated by

Katie Gamb

My name is Elizabeth.

I am someone who does her homework before being told; I love arts and crafts, give my stuffed animals makeovers and like things tidy.

This is my dad. He spends hours looking at baseball numbers, thinks he's pretty funny and has his own way of doing things.

This is my little sister, Lulu. She is just, so, so, Lulu.

WAKE

When I spend the day with my dad, things can be ...
a little different.

UP, DAD!

Like, sometimes I am the alarm clock!

Sometimes we eat an unusual breakfast.

Sometimes my bed gets made,
but it looks like someone is still in it.

"Lulu?"

Once Lulu's shoes went on the wrong feet,

but not for the entire day.

Sometimes my pigtails look   like a pig put them in.

Dad is hopeless at helping with my art projects.

But he thinks everything I do is a masterpiece.

Nap time can turn into TICKLE time,

and Dad is always the clumsiest guest at our tea parties.

When I am with Dad, I have to use the **wrong** bathroom.

START

Sometimes my room looks like an obstacle course!

On some days we "get" to watch the game.

Our bath time can turn into a water park.

My dad makes up the best, craziest bedtime stories.

Some nights, all of my tricks to avoid going to bed work, but I end up falling asleep anyway.